ISBN 0-590-28286-7

Copyright © 1989 by Jez Alborough.
All rights reserved.
Published by Scholastic Inc., 555 Broadway, New York, NY 10012,
by arrangement with Candlewick Press.
SCHOLASTIC and associated logos are trademarks
and/or registered trademarks of Scholastic Inc.

12 11 10 9 8 7 6 5 4 3 2 1   8 9/9 0 1 2 3/0

Printed in the U.S.A.   23

First Scholastic printing, January 1998

This book was typeset in New Baskerville.
The pictures were done in watercolor and pencil.

ICE CREAM

BEAR

JEZ ALBOROUGH

SCHOLASTIC INC.
New York Toronto London Auckland Sydney

Bear should fix that broken pane—

it dribbles drops of snow and rain.

But jobs like that are always kept
till after lazy Bear has slept.

He dreams of slipping out the back

to fetch himself an icy snack.

But what a shock when he gets there,

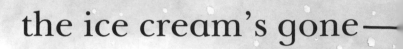

the ice cream's gone—

the cupboard's bare!

As he turns and starts to shout,

a pile of snow falls on his snout.

At least, that is, he thinks it's snow.
It feels too thick and sticky, though,

and tastes of sugar. Can it mean . . .

it's snowing blobs of white ice cream?

It's twice as nice as snow or ice;

it's Bear's idea of paradise.

Before he tries to eat it all,

he makes himself a little ball,

then rolls it into something grand . . .

the biggest scoop

in all the land!

But suddenly it starts to slip,

and Bear begins to lose his grip.

Now it's time without delay . . .

to make a speedy getaway.

He sees a rock—too late to dodge—

rolls over once, and . . .

WATCH OUT!

SPLODGE!

"Ice cream!" he screams.
"Ice cream, ice cream!

Thank heavens, it was all a dream."

Now he does not hesitate;
the household chores will have to wait.

Broken windows should be fixed . . .

but work and pleasure
can't be mixed.